How to Become a Calypsonian

Written by Desryn T. A. Collins

Illustrated by Richy Sanchez Ayala

Collins

My name is Mighty Glen Glen ...

Hi. My name is Mighty Glen Glen. I am a singer.
I sing a special kind of song called a **calypso**. I am
the Calypso King at my school.

When I am singing a calypso, I clap, dance, jump, talk
and walk around the stage. I am a mighty performer,
so I call myself "Mighty Glen Glen". My real name is
Glenroy Jones.

I bet you can be a mighty performer too.

It's not hard to become a calypsonian. I helped my friend Donnette to become a calypsonian. I'll tell you what I told her.

Anyone can become a calypsonian if they like to tell stories and sing. A calypso is a story that is sung. Let me tell you a little more about calypsos.

Calypso, sweet calypso

Calypsos are songs with a lively beat. People in Africa first started singing this type of song, but they did not call their songs calypsos. I like that word – "calypso"! I have tried to find where this name for the song originally came from, but no one knows for sure.

It could be from Africa. It could be from France. It could be from Spain.

The word "calypso" could be from just about anywhere! But a calypso is definitely a sweet tropical song that came from Africa.

CARIBBEAN

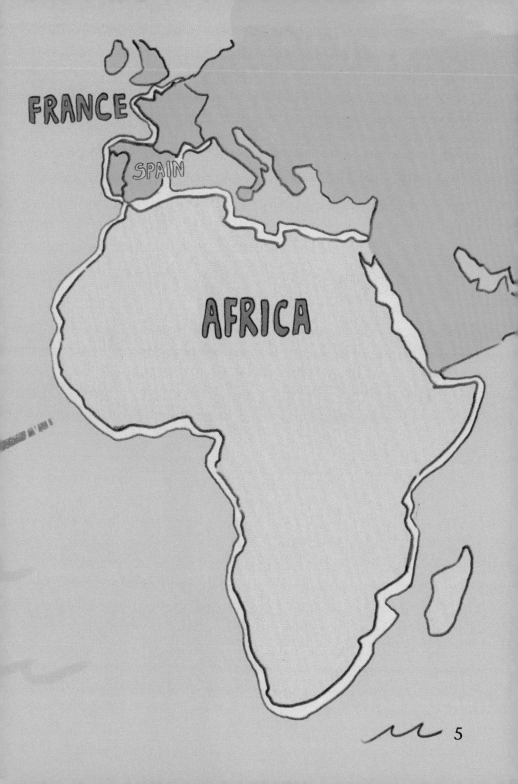

FRANCE

SPAIN

AFRICA

5

A calypso is called a tropical song because it is popular in all the **Caribbean** islands, but not only Caribbean people sing calypsos. People all around the world also know about calypsos and they enjoy this type of music. Calypsos are so sweet, people just can't help liking them.

You have to tell your story in a lively, enchanting song.
Long ago, people in West Africa did that too.
They told a story in a song which was called a **Kaiso**.
The African Kaiso music is what evolved into
the calypso. My grandfather told me all about the
origin of calypso music. I think it's super interesting!

But when and where did people in the Caribbean start singing calypsos? Most likely, people started to sing calypsos in Trinidad in the first half of the 19th century. The lyrics, which are the words in the songs, told stories about what was happening in the society. The songs were important because, for many people, this was the only way for them to know what was taking place.

Calypsos still tell stories. The calypsonian performs on stage with a group of musicians playing different instruments. These instruments are mainly **congas**, **claves**, **jugs**, spoons, **bongos**, classical guitar, bass guitar, trumpet, trombone, flute, saxophone, **bamboo sticks,** violin, clarinet, **maracas** and the **steelpan**. The instruments help to make calypso music very special.

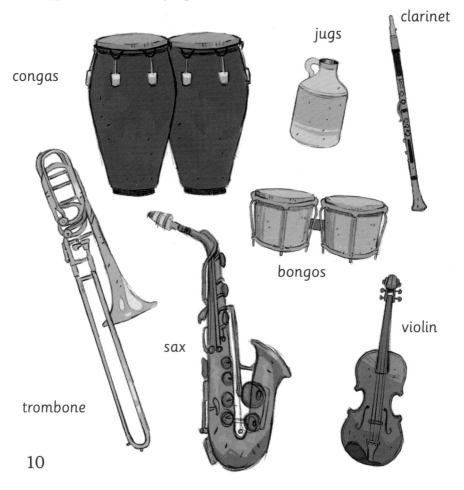

clarinet

jugs

congas

bongos

violin

sax

trombone

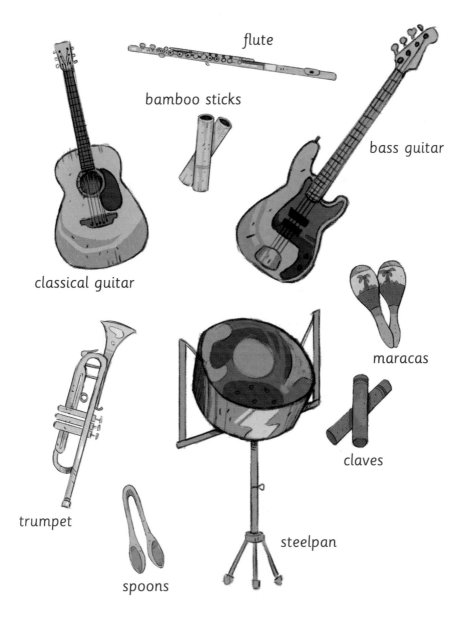

flute

bamboo sticks

bass guitar

classical guitar

maracas

trumpet

claves

spoons

steelpan

So, do you want to make sweet, sweet calypso music?
It's easy! These are the steps I took.

Step one: be very observant

First, I watched what was going on at school, in my
street and everywhere I went around the country.
I also listened to everything. I listened to what
the adults were talking about and what was on
the news. I was as curious as a little kitten! I listened
to my friends, and I wanted to know what
the neighbours were talking about too. Wow!
People were talking about so much!

Some people discussed pollution and politicians, others talked about care for the elderly, children complained about bullying, and many people talked about the rights of boys and girls. It was fascinating and I was learning a lot!

Step two: choose a topic and plan your calypso

Something that you hear about while you are watching and listening to everything around you will make you very excited. That's what you should write your calypso about. Once you have chosen your topic, start planning your song.

Step three: write your calypso

Once you have decided on your topic, that's when the fun starts!

It's time to choose tricky words.

You have to make words rhyme.

Toss in some colourful adjectives.

Let your verbs sizzle!

You might spend a lot of time writing because, to win the crown, you have to get your calypso just right.

The verses of the song take the form of a poem which is called a **ballad**. Ballads are stories which are told in verses or **stanzas**. A typical calypso has a stanza of eight lines which is followed by a chorus which has four lines. Each stanza gives more details about the story that the calypsonian is telling. There are at least three stanzas and a chorus which follows each stanza in the calypso.

It sounds challenging but I know you can master it.

The calypsonian has to be very clever. I wrote my story very carefully so that no one was upset by what I sang.

Bully Dog

One day as I was walk– ing feel– ing, hap– py and care– free – I

saw a kit– ten scram– bling up a big tam– a– rind tree. I

did– n't hear it cry– ing – it looked quite fine to me, But

then I heard the bark– ing that caused the kit– ten to flee. I

turned to that A– ki– ta, ve– ry se– ri– ous was my tone: Go

home to yuh "own– na"– leave the poor kit– ty a– lone. Go

home, old A– ki– ta, don't cause more strife. You make young kit–ty shi–ver– stop

mess– ing with its life.

Are you ready to give it a try?

You can sing about animals when you really mean to talk about people. You have to choose the right words. If you put in what people say, try to write the words in the way you hear them spoken. Make your song funny, but make your listeners think about something important.

Step four: practise your calypso

The next step is to practise your calypso. I practised at school with the other calypsonians in my school's competition. Calypsonians usually go to a place called a **calypso tent** to practise for competitions. The calypso tent is a real tent or a building where calypsonians gather to practise and it is also where competitions are held.

CALYPSO TENT

A lot of people gather in a calypso tent. These people are calypsonians and their musicians, as well as other people who like calypsos. They share ideas with the calypsonians while they are practising. It's great fun!

You'll get advice on how to make your song better. Making changes can be hard, but I learnt that it's worth the effort. Sometimes you might change a word, or a sentence or a whole stanza! You also have to practise your gestures and movement. The timing of your music has to be perfect too.

Step five: choose your stage name

Before the performance, you have to choose a special stage name. Choose a name that is catchy. Very soon, everyone will be calling you by your special stage name. Everybody calls me Mighty Glen Glen!

Most calypsonians have names with two parts. For the first part of the name, they choose words such as: mighty, lord, king, lady, baby, queen, calypso and chief. The second part is a nickname that the singer likes. Some calypsonians choose single word names. I can't wait to hear what name you choose!

Step six: perform the calypso

At last, it will be the day of the Calypso Monarch Competition. You will be very excited to get on stage to perform your calypso. This is the final step. You might feel a little jittery from nerves, but don't worry, you'll be fine once you start performing.

Winning the crown is every calypsonian's dream.
Dressed in stunning outfits, they get on stage
and perform confidently. That's what you'll have
to do if you want to win.

While you are performing, the judges will pay keen attention to the lyrics of the song, how well the music was arranged and how you use the stage.

The performer who impresses the judges the most is chosen to be the Calypso Monarch. Every year, only one person gets the crown, but everyone who performs is very happy to be a calypsonian.

I know you'll be a great performer. Just follow my steps and the crown will be yours. I bet you can't wait to get started. Put on your curiosity cap. Soon, you'll be singing and dancing like me – your favourite calypsonian, the Mighty Glen Glen!

Glossary

ballad
a form of poetry that tells a story

bamboo sticks
thin pieces of bamboo pole from the bamboo tree which are hit together to make a musical sound

bongos
a pair of small open-bottomed drums, which are native to Cuba

calypso
a tropical song with a lively beat. The song tells an interesting story about a topic people care about.

calypso tent
an actual tent or building where calypsonians meet to practise their calypsos, especially in preparation for a big competition, such as a Calypso Monarch Competition during carnival season

Caribbean
a group of islands which are found in the Caribbean Sea

claves
a pair of sticks about 20-30 millimetres thick, which are used to make music

congas   tall, narrow drums that are played by themselves or to back up a musician

jugs   empty jugs can be used as a musical instrument to make a low hoarse sound

Kaiso   a style of music that can be traced back to West Africa. The singer is joined by musicians playing a number of traditional instruments.

maracas   musical instruments made of gourds which have pebbles or seeds in them. They have a wooden handle. Music is made by shaking or rattling two gourds.

stanzas   sets of lines that form sections of a poem or song

steelpan   a musical instrument that was created in Trinidad and Tobago. It is made from a metal drum. The musician, who is called a pannist, beats the drum to make the music.

How to become a calypsonian

Be observant.

Select a subject and plan the calypso.

Write the calypso.

Perform the calypso.

Choose your stage name.

Practise the calypso.

Ideas for reading

Written by Christine Whitney
Primary Literacy Consultant

Reading objectives:
- read for a range of purposes
- be introduced to different structures in non-fiction books
- retrieve information from non-fiction

Spoken language objectives:
- ask relevant questions
- speculate, imagine and explore ideas through talk
- participate in discussions

Curriculum links: Music - children perform, listen to and evaluate music across a range of historical periods, genres, styles and traditions; Writing - write for different purposes and audiences

Word count: 1398

Interest words: calypso, ballad, stanza, congas, bongos, claves

Resources: a variety of instruments as labelled on pages 10 and 11

Build a context for reading

- Show children a selection of musical instruments used in calypso music. Ask children to name them and to discuss if they know how to play them.

- Ask children to share their understanding of what a calypso is. Listen to some calypso music.

- Ask children if they know how to become a calypso singer – *a calypsonian*. Have they ever seen any calypso singers perform live?